Classics for Beginning Readers

Reader's Digest Young Families

The Tale of Mrs. Tiggy-Winkle

Designer: Wendy Boccuzzi and Elaine Lopez
Editor: Sharon Yates
Editorial Director: Pamela Pia

Adapted text by Margaret Snyder copyright © 2003 Reader's Digest Young Families, Inc.
Based on the original story written by Beatrix Potter.
Illustrations by Maggie Swanson copyright © 2003 Reader's Digest Young Families, Inc.

The Classics for Beginning Readers logo and Reader's Digest Young Families
are registered trademarks of The Reader's Digest Association, Inc.

Printed in China.

Reader's Digest Young Families

The Tale of Mrs. Tiggy-Winkle

Based on the story written in 1905

by

Beatrix Potter

Retold by Margaret Snyder

Illustrations by
Maggie Swanson

Once there was a little girl named Lucy who lived on a farm. Lucy was a good little girl, but she was always losing things.

One morning when Lucy was playing, she reached for her handkerchief.

"Oh, dear!" said Lucy, when she saw it was gone. "That is the third hankie I have lost. I just have to find it!"

Lucy looked all over for her hankie, but she did not see it anywhere.

"Have you seen my hankie, Tabby Kitten?" she asked the farm cat. The cat didn't answer. She just kept licking her paws.

Next, Lucy asked the hen. "Have you seen my hankie, Sally Henny-Penny?"

The hen clucked something that sounded like, "I go barefoot, barefoot, barefoot!" With that, the hen turned and ran into the barn.

Just then, Lucy heard the robin singing.
"Mr. Robin, have you seen my hankie?" she
asked. The robin flew off chirping as if telling
Lucy to follow him. Up, up the hill the robin
went. And up, up the hill ran Lucy.

Finally the bird landed on a low stone wall. Lucy sat down and looked around. Close by, she could see a bubbling brook. "What's that?" Lucy thought as she looked at the mud. It was a tiny bucket surrounded by a trail of tiny footprints.

Lucy followed the footprints to a clearing, where she found a clothesline made out of plant stems. There was also a door built right into the hill. Behind the door someone was singing:

"*Lily-white and clean, oh!*
With little frills between, oh!
Smooth and hot — red, rusty spot!
Never here be seen, oh!"

Lucy knocked. "Come in," said a small voice. The little girl carefully ducked through the tiny doorway. She found herself in a very small kitchen. There were pots hanging from the ceiling, and there were two tidy baskets of clothes on the floor. In the middle of the room was the strangest little woman Lucy had ever seen.

The little woman's black nose went sniffle, sniffle, sniffle, and her eyes went twinkle, twinkle, twinkle. Then she straightened her apron and her petticoats and said to Lucy, "Hello, my name is Mrs. Tiggy-Winkle. I am an excellent clothes washer."

Mrs. Tiggy-Winkle took something red out of her clothes basket and began to iron it. "Is that my handkerchief?" Lucy asked, trying not to stare at the funny hairpins sticking out of the woman's white cap.

"No. This is Mr. Robin's scarlet vest," answered Mrs. Tiggy-Winkle.

Again Mrs. Tiggy-Winkle's nose went sniffle, sniffle, sniffle, and her eyes went twinkle, twinkle, twinkle. Then she took out another piece from the wash basket. "My hankie!" Lucy cried.

"So it is," said Mrs. Tiggy-Winkle as she pressed and folded the hankie for Lucy.

Next, Mrs. Tiggy-Winkle took from the basket two long yellow things with fingers like gloves. "These are Sally Henny-Penny's stockings," she said. Lucy's mouth dropped open in surprise. Sally had been trying to tell her about Mrs. Tiggy-Winkle when she had clucked about going barefoot.

Lucy pointed to some funny white things hanging up to dry. "They are Tabby Kitten's mittens," said Mrs. Tiggy-Winkle. "I only have to iron them, though. She washes them by herself."

Lucy giggled. "Mrs. Tiggy-Winkle was right," Lucy thought. "The cat was always licking her paws."

Just then Mrs. Tiggy-Winkle pulled out two more handkerchiefs from the wash basket.

"My other hankies!" Lucy said with amazement. The washerwoman smiled as she pressed and folded them. Then she took all three hankies and neatly pinned them to the inside of Lucy's jacket.

At last, Mrs. Tiggy-Winkle's wash basket was empty. "The ironing is finished," she said. "Time to dry the clothes." She took an armful of damp clothes from another basket and went outside to hang them on the line. "This tailcoat with no tail is Squirrel Nutkin's, and this shrunken jacket belongs to Peter Rabbit," Mrs. Tiggy-Winkle explained.

After hanging up the clothes, Mrs. Tiggy-Winkle poured some tea. That's when Lucy noticed the tiny woman's brown and wrinkly hands. And even stranger were her hairpins. Not only did they stick out of the woman's white cap, they poked through her clothing too!

When tea time was over, Mrs. Tiggy-Winkle
went straight back to work. She sorted the clothes
and tied them into neat bundles. Then she picked
up the bundles and trotted down the hill. Lucy
followed close behind.

As Lucy and Mrs. Tiggy-Winkle walked down the path, little animals came out to greet them. Peter Rabbit and Benjamin Bunny were the first. They took their bundles of clothes from Mrs. Tiggy-Winkle and thanked her again and again. Mr. Robin flew down to get his red vest, singing out his thanks.

Soon all of the bundles were gone, and it was time for Lucy to go home. But when Lucy turned to say good-bye and thank the kind washerwoman for finding her hankies, Mrs. Tiggy-Winkle started running up the hill!

Lucy stared at Mrs. Tiggy-Winkle. The little washerwoman now had no white cap, no apron and no petticoats. She had become smaller and brown and was covered with prickles. "Why, Mrs. Tiggy-Winkle! You are a hedgehog!" Lucy said with surprise.

When Lucy returned home and told her family about Mrs. Tiggy-Winkle, they said she must have been dreaming. But if it was just a dream, how did the three missing hankies turn up cleaned, pressed and pinned to the inside of Lucy's jacket?